. . . for parents and teachers

In *Why Do I Daydream?*, Betty Ren Wright deals with a favorite pastime of children and others — daydreaming. This story highlights the point that daydreaming is fun and normal, but that reality also has its advantages, including bringing satisfaction to others besides oneself.

Childhood daydreaming and fantasy-building can certainly be frustrating to adults. In this story, Alex dreams of fame and superhuman skills, only to find the adults around her impatient with her "lackadaisical" attitude.

And yet, her behavior serves a useful purpose. She gets a chance to dream about her future and step into exciting situations. While parents and teachers may often become annoyed or angered by such activities, we must acknowledge their value and hesitate before overreacting. We must trust our children to work through these fantasies while maintaining a base in reality. Providing such support and encouragement presents us with quite a challenge.

In fact, this story reminds me of my latest case, which is just such a challenge. The children of the world have united and contacted me to assist in negotiating their family problems about daydreaming . . . . Thank you, Betty Ren Wright — wherever you are.

MANUEL S. SILVERMAN, Ph.D.
ASSOCIATE PROFESSOR
DEPARTMENT OF GUIDANCE AND
    COUNSELING
LOYOLA UNIVERSITY OF CHICAGO

Betty Ren Wright is the author
of over forty books for children.
She lives in Wisconsin.

Copyright © 1991 Steck-Vaughn Company

Library of Congress Number: 80-25561

8 9 10 11 12   93 92 91

Library of Congress Cataloging in Publication Data

Wright, Betty·Ren.
  Why do I daydream?

  SUMMARY: While running an errand during a snowstorm,
Alexandra, a daydreamer, finds that reality also has its
advantages.
  I. Redman, Tom.   II. Title
PZ7.W933Wh   (Fic.)   80-25561
ISBN 0-8172-1371-6 lib. bdg.

WHY DO I DAYDREAM?

by Betty Ren Wright

illustrated by Tom Redman

introduction by Manuel S. Silverman, Ph.D.

RAINTREE
STECK-VAUGHN
L I B R A R Y
A Division of Steck-Vaughn Company

I don't like to be called daydreamer. It's true — I *am* usually thinking about something or other most of the time. But when people call me a daydreamer, they make it sound like thinking is *bad*.

One day last winter, all I could think about was being able to fly. The world was so beautiful. The big snowstorm was over. Snow had drifted up to our windows.

And we were out of milk.

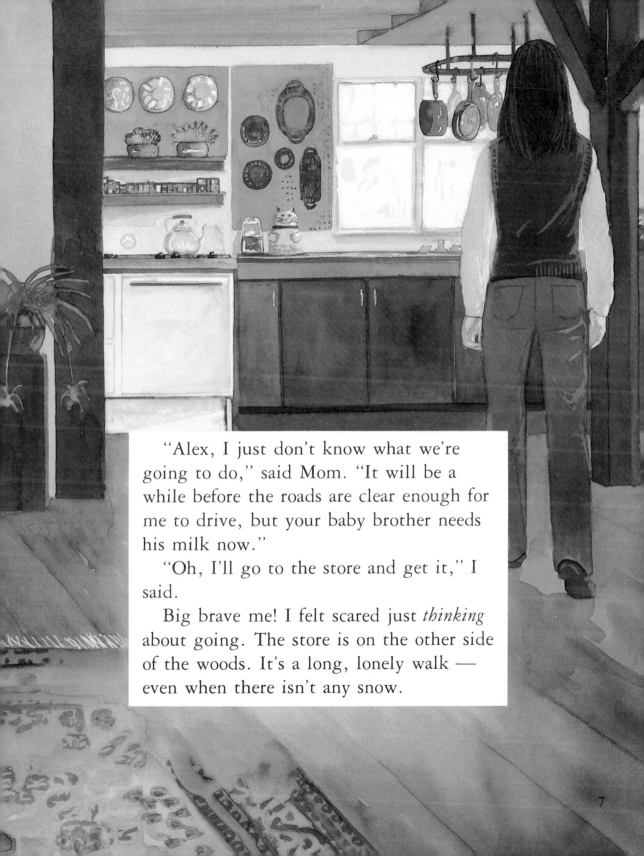

"Alex, I just don't know what we're going to do," said Mom. "It will be a while before the roads are clear enough for me to drive, but your baby brother needs his milk now."

"Oh, I'll go to the store and get it," I said.

Big brave me! I felt scared just *thinking* about going. The store is on the other side of the woods. It's a long, lonely walk — even when there isn't any snow.

I started to put on my coat. Then I took out my list of Super-Great Daydreams. I make out a new list every week or so. I like to look at it every day, to see if any of the daydreams might be coming true.

That day it looked like this:

1. Get a dog and call him Barney.
2. Do something brave enough to win a medal.
3. Ride my bike faster than anyone else in my class.
4. Fly like Superman.

That last one was pretty silly, but I really liked it. It would be so great to zoom over the treetops. . . .

"Alexandra, aren't you dressed yet?"
Mom called from the kitchen. "I hope
you're not in there daydreaming." She's
always after me about my daydreaming.

I sat down to pull on my boots. A dog
would really help on a trip like this, I was
thinking. He could carry the milk in a
special bag on his back. . . .

Suddenly Mom was right behind me. I thought she would be really angry. But instead she said, "I wish you wouldn't daydream so much. Come on, you'd better go before it starts getting dark."

Quickly I put on my hat and mittens. Mom gave me a hug, and we pushed on the back door until it opened enough for me to slip outside.

"If you get too tired, come back," Mom called.

Before I even reached the woods, I knew what a hard trip this was going to be. The snow was higher than my knees. It tugged at my boots.

When I got to the end of our yard, I turned and waved to Mom. I was glad she couldn't hear me puffing.

The snow in the woods was deep and smooth. Squirrels looked down and scolded me. A rabbit hopped ahead.

"Lucky rabbit," I said. "Sure wish I could *fly*!"

It seemed like forever before I came to
the road that was the halfway point. The
air was so cold that it hurt to breathe. I
stood for a minute and looked down the
white road. There was nothing to see. But
way off there was a small black spot — so
far away I couldn't tell what it was.

I was tired. I found a log to sit on. The
woods were so quiet. High above me, a
bird soared. I thought about what it would
be like to be that bird. I would really see
how the countryside looked — all white
and full of strange snow-covered shapes.

Then snow began to fall again — the stinging, blowing kind that hurts your face.

"Hey!" I said. I was surprised, and also mad at myself. I didn't know how long I had been sitting there, but now I really felt cold. Why, oh *why*, did I daydream?

I wanted to cry. But I got up and started walking. At last I saw the store.

It's a nice store, warm and full of good
smells. I sat down on a box and rested.
The storekeeper gave me an apple to eat.
He put the milk carton in a bag and gave
it to me.

Finally he said, "Alexandra, you'd better
stop your daydreaming and get moving.
There's not much daylight left."

I started back.

It was snowing harder than ever. The
wind tried to knock me over. Snow crept
inside my collar and down my boots. My
feet ached with cold.

At last I reached the road again.
"Halfway!" I said. But I was too tired to
care. I didn't even feel like daydreaming. I
just wanted to sleep.

I looked down the road. The black spot
I'd seen before was only a few feet away
from me now. It was a dog! He looked lost
and scared and as cold as I was.

"Good dog. Good Barney," I called. He
came right up to me, his short tail
wagging. He had no collar or tags. I
picked him up. He was shivering.

After that, a strange thing happened.
Even though the dog was kind of heavy, I
walked faster. I didn't stumble. I talked to
him and forgot all about my cold feet.
Before I knew it, I had come out of the
woods and into my backyard.

I was home!

After Mom fed the baby, she built a big
fire in the fireplace. We put Barney in
front of it, and then we drank cocoa and
played with him.

"You know what?" I said. "My Number
One Super-Great Daydream just came true.
I have a dog called Barney."

"You know what else?" Mom said. "I
think you were a real hero today, Alex.
You kept on going right through all that
snow. You got the milk, and you saved
Barney. You ought to have a medal for
being so brave."

Wow, I thought. *There's Daydream
Number Two!*

That left Number Three. I made up my
mind to start practicing on my bike as
soon as the snow melted.

And then there was Number Four —
learning to fly like Superman. I decided to
cross that one off my list. Sure, it would
be great to fly. But I didn't think it was
the most important thing in the world
anymore. I was kind of proud of *walking*
through all that snow.

Besides, if I'd been zooming over the
treetops that day, I probably never would
have found Barney.